In the Danger Zone

Dear Reader

If you step into an animal's danger zone, you might be stung, poisoned, eaten, spiked, needled, bitten or killed.

AUSTRALIA HAS THE TOP TEN VENOMOUS SNAKES IN THE WORLD!

One of the most deadly creatures is so small you can hardly see it – the malaria-spreading mosquito – find out more about it on pages 8 and 9.

Another almost invisible creature will cause you agonising pain if you brush against it – the box jellyfish – pages 12 and 13 will tell you more.

I hope you're amazed and more informed when you read about some of the deadly and very dangerous zones!

Sharon Parsons

NELSON
CENGAGE Learning™
For learning solutions, visit cengage.com.au

Contents

In the DANGER ZONE

What's a Danger Zone?

Dangerous When Threatened

The area around an animal may become a danger zone for other animals and humans.

If an animal feels threatened, it will defend itself.

VERTEBRATE: REPTILE
puff adder

A Snake's Danger Zone

Imagine a snake snoozing in the sun. If it senses a predator invading its zone, its instinct is to slide away. If its path is blocked, it will defend itself.

Enter the snake's danger zone and you risk getting a snakebite.

INVERTEBRATE: INSECT
red bull ant

Keep CLEAR of the **DANGER ZONES!**

GER
NES

A Bull Ant's Danger Zone

Look down at the ground and you might see a large bull ant walking among smaller ants. The bull ant will only sting you if you get in its way.

Stay clear of the bull ant's danger zone.
It can sting over and over again!

A Jellyfish's Danger Zone

Swim in areas where jellyfish live and you may be entering their danger zone – near their tentacles.

Keep clear of the jellyfish's danger zone.
You risk painful stings that could kill you or make you ill.

Not all jellyfish are dangerous to humans.

INVERTEBRATE: MARINE
sea nettle jellyfish

Deadly and Dangerous Animals

The World's Deadliest Animals

A crocodile snaps up for attack.

When deadly animals sense danger in the zone around them, they may attack.

A snake sprays venom.

Natural Instinct

Their natural instinct is to protect themselves and their young in order to survive.

Remember that animals only become deadly and dangerous towards us if we enter their danger zone.

A jellyfish stings.

A scorpion bites.

ATTACK!

Top Ten Most Deadly Animals

Ten of the most deadly animals in the world for humans are the:

1. mosquito
2. venomous snake
3. scorpion
4. large cat (lion, cougar)
5. crocodile
6. elephant
7. hippopotamus
8. jellyfish
9. shark
10. bear.

Note: Each country may have a different list of top ten most deadly animals.

A bear growls.

A hippopotamus crushes.

A mosquito bites.

Elephants charge.

A great white shark bites.

A lion roars.

The MOST Dangerous Zones!

Danger Zones in the Air

Location

Malaria-spreading mosquitoes live in over 100 countries – mainly in Africa, Asia, the Middle East and South America. For people in those places, the danger zones are their homes and villages.

Figures

Every year about 250 million people suffer from malaria. About one million of those people die from malaria each year – most of them are children.

Affordable Malaria Cure for Poor Families

New funding would help to lower the cost of malaria drugs for poor families. In Africa and Asia, about 900 000 children die each year from malaria.

The cost could be as low as 20 cents per treatment for poor families to buy the malaria drugs, which use the sweet wormwood herb. This herb helps to prevent and treat malaria.

sweet wormwood herb
(*Artemisia annua*)

Life Science and Health

The Mosquito's Life Cycle

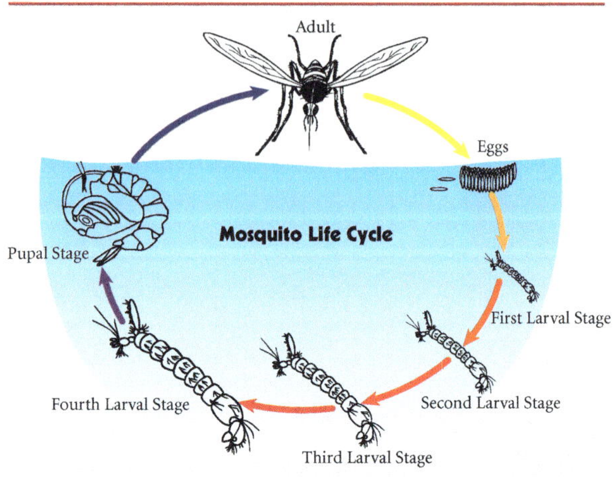

The Disease

Malaria is a tiny parasite. It only lives in the bodies of female mosquitoes. When the mosquito bites a human, it injects a tiny amount of saliva to keep blood flowing through the bite. Sometimes, malaria parasites can be injected into the person with this saliva.

The malaria parasites grow in the person's blood. If that person is bitten by another mosquito, the malaria parasites may enter this new mosquito.

The new mosquito may then inject malaria parasites into other people. That's how malaria can spread.

NOT ALL MOSQUITOES CARRY MALARIA.

The Danger

Most people don't know they have been infected with malaria for months or even years afterwards. In that time, mosquitoes can infect other people around their area, too. Malaria can make people feel very ill or, in time, kill them.

Best Prevention

Before going to countries where malaria mosquitoes live, see a doctor. Take medication before, during and after your visit.

Extra Prevention

In the early mornings and evenings, wear clothes to cover most of your body. Wear an insect repellent on any bare skin.

The Most **Dangerous Zones on Land**

Location

Most countries have snakes. Some of the countries with *no* snakes are: New Zealand, Ireland, Iceland and Greenland.

NOT ALL SNAKES ARE VENOMOUS OR HARMFUL TO PEOPLE.

Figures

The World Health Organisation (WHO) estimates that about one million people are bitten by snakes each year and up to 40 000 people die. There are about 2000 species of snake and about 450 species are venomous.

AMAZING SNAKE FACTS

A Most Colourful Snake: Brazilian Rainbow Boa

Smallest Snake: A thread snake can be 10cm long!

Longest Snake: Scrub pythons can grow to 5.65 metres.

Most Poisonous Snakes: Sea snakes are more poisonous than land snakes – rarely bite or inject much venom.

Biggest Fangs: The taipan's fangs can grow to more than 12 millimetres.

Most Venom: The mulga snake holds a world record for the most venom.

The Dangers

Different snakes have different venoms. People may experience different symptoms. They may feel dizzy or sick; they may have blurry vision; they may have trouble breathing. People may be paralysed.

The Venom

Venom is a type of poisonous saliva. A snake can inject venom into its prey, using its sharp fangs like needles. The venom spreads throughout the body in the "lymph".

Best Prevention

Before going to countries or areas where venomous snakes live, find out how to identify those snakes. Ask a doctor for first-aid advice on how to treat snakebites. At home, practise treating a snakebite on someone in your family.

Extra Prevention

Stay away from places where snakes may be resting, such as sunny rocks and behind logs. When walking in the bush, check the sides of paths. If you spot a snake, back away slowly and do not disturb it at all.

THE LYMPHATIC SYSTEM

Lymph is a fluid that collects waste from our tissues and takes it to lymph nodes or glands in our neck, under our arms and other parts of the body. Then lymph fluid returns to the blood.

Life Science and Health

Top Ten Venomous Snakes

Australia has the top ten most venomous snakes in the world! The most venomous land snake has three different names – the inland taipan, small-scaled snake or fierce snake.

The Most **Dangerous Zones** in the **Sea**

Location

Throughout the world's oceans, there are many dangerous zones. One of the worst danger zones for people is around deadly jellyfish. The most deadly are the box jellyfish or jellyfish stingers.

JELLYFISH STINGERS

Made of over 95 per cent water, the jellyfish has no head, brain, heart, ears or bones. But something this creature does have is tentacles armed with poisonous stinging cells.

Figures

It is estimated that about 100 people worldwide die each year from box jellyfish stings.

Life Science and Health

Box Jellyfish

The box jellyfish actively hunts its prey, rather than drifting as other jellyfish do. Some marine species, such as sea turtles, are immune to the venom and are known to feed on the jellyfish.

a sea turtle

NOT ALL JELLYFISH ARE DANGEROUS TO HUMANS.

The Venom

The box jellyfish has about 60 long, stinging tentacles. It uses these to inject venom into its prey. As soon as a fish – or an unlucky human – touches a tentacle, the jellyfish shoots out tiny, poisonous stings. It can be very painful!

The Danger

Box jellyfish are hard to see. They are light blue and almost see-through.

If a box jellyfish stings a person, that person could die within minutes.

Best Care

Get out of the water quickly and seek medical help immediately. Wash the sting and surrounding area with vinegar. This stops any more venom being released into the skin.

Extra Care

Find out the "stinger season" danger months.

SWIMMING DANGER

Do not swim in any area where dangerous species of jellyfish swim.

Do not swim close to, or touch, any jellyfish – even dead ones on the shore.

A Danger Zone for a Snake

A **Cane Toad** Takes on a **Snake!**

In 2008, a female cane toad was found eating its predator – the keelback snake! The snake entered the poisonous cane toad's danger zone!

The non-venomous keelback snake can eat poisonous cane toads and still survive. Cane toad experts were hoping that the snakes could help reduce the huge numbers of cane toads.

Graeme Sawyer

Making the News

FrogWatch NT Coordinator and Darwin Lord Mayor, Graeme Sawyer, told the *Northern Territory News* that he found a cane toad eating a keelback snake at their cane toad research area, 100 kilometres south of Darwin, Australia.

History and Life Science

Poisonous Cane Toads

In 1935, 3000 cane toads were brought to Australia to control a pest – the cane beetle that was destroying sugar cane crops. The toads ate the beetles, but Australia ended up with an even more serious problem.

Cane toads are poisonous and can breed very quickly. A female can lay up to 30 000 eggs at a time. Thousands of toads have invaded Northern Australia, Queensland and parts of New South Wales.

An Excerpt from the *Northern Territory News*

a cane toad eating a keelback snake

Graeme Sawyer said about one-sixth of the 60-centimetre snake was down the toad's throat.

"I was absolutely amazed," he said.

"To see a large female cane toad eating a live snake is unbelievable."

Mr Sawyer said he removed the snake from the toad's mouth and somehow it was still alive, so he released it into nearby bushland. As for the cane toad, it's still alive at the cane toad research area.

Mr Sawyer said the fact that a cane toad took on a snake raised the question, *"What are these animals doing to our wildlife and our biodiversity?"*

Mr Sawyer said that cane toads are causing huge problems to Northern Territory wildlife and not just the animals that die from eating cane toads.

"We've found a range of animals inside the stomachs of cane toads as part of our research – centipedes, scorpions and spiders have been some of the most common," he said. *"It's a big concern."*

5 Is the Great Barrier Reef a Danger Zone?

The World's **Largest** Coral **Reef**

The Great Barrier Reef is the largest coral reef in the world. It's also the world's largest super-organism. The reef has the largest collection of organisms living in it, as well as many more living on and around it.

CORAL

Coral is a living organism.

Is the Great Barrier Reef a Danger Zone?

The reef can be a danger zone for people who dive and snorkel around it. If divers and snorkellers explore the reef with skilled guides, they will have a safer and more enjoyable time. The reef will be protected, too.

the Great Barrier Reef

What Are Some of the **Reef's Dangers?**

Blue-Ringed Octopus

This octopus is very dangerous. There is no known antidote for its venomous sting. When this octopus feels threatened, the rings on its skin glow bright blue and it becomes more dangerous. Usually, it is shy and won't attack unless it is touched or stepped on.

a blue-ringed octopus

Box Jellyfish

Box jellyfish are one of the deadliest creatures in the shallow waters of the reef.

a cone shell snail

Cone Shell Snails

If a cone shell snail is touched, its sting can be venomous to people.

Irukandji Jellyfish

This small jellyfish, the size of a fingernail, can be found in deep waters around the reef.

Turn the page for more reef dangers ... if you dare!

Sea Snakes

There are many species of sea snake on the reef. They are the most venomous snake on Earth! They're not likely to attack people, but be careful.

Stingrays

The barbs on a stingray's tail can cause serious cuts and wounds. This is a very dangerous zone for people.

stingrays

a lionfish

Stonefish

The poisonous spines of stonefish can cause pain and kill body tissue. At low tide, stonefish hide on the sea floor, so wear shoes with strong soles for walking along the beach.

Lionfish

Lionfish have venomous spines that can cause painful wounds.

IS THE **CROWN-OF-THORNS** UPSETTING THE REEF'S ECOSYSTEM?

The crown-of-thorns starfish feed on the reef's coral. In small numbers, they are harmless. But if their numbers continue to increase, they will end up eating the coral faster than it can grow.

Even the world's biggest super-organism can be threatened by an outbreak of this starfish.

And that upsets the ecosystem of the Great Barrier Reef.

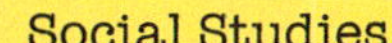

a crown-of-thorns starfish

Social Studies

Do People Upset the Reef's Ecosystem?

Yes. People are damaging the reef. Run-off from farms can pollute the water with pesticides and fertilisers. Sediment clouds the water. Climate change appears to be making the sea more acidic, and acid can dissolve coral.

Science Feature
A Jellyfish Breeding Program

an adult moon jellyfish showing a few of its four stomach rings

The Melbourne Aquarium in Australia breeds moon jellyfish (moon jellies). They start life as tiny polyps, which grow into what look like little sea anemones. The polyps are kept at 14–16° Celsius in a birthing tank. When the temperature changes, the polyps bud to form new tiny jellyfish.

Jelly Babies Grow Up

The baby moon jellies are kept in a bigger tank and feed on plankton. In four weeks they are as big as a 50-cent coin and in four to five months they become adults.

Moon Jellies Location

These see-through jellies are almost invisible in the world's oceans. Vast numbers of them live along the Western Australian coast and in Perth's Swan River.

Di collects food for the moon jellies.

Helping Jellyfish to Breed

Sea jellies expert Di Brandl breeds moon jellies at the Melbourne Aquarium. That means there is always a supply of these jellyfish, even in winter, when there are few in the wild.

6 Plants with Danger Zones!

From **Stinging Nettle** to **Deadly Berries**

Many plants are danger zones for people – we shouldn't pick or eat any parts of plants unless we know they are safe. Always check with an adult if you're unsure.

Stay Away from Stinging Nettles

If your skin touches the stinging nettle's leaves and stems, you will feel a sharp, stinging pain. This can last for hours. A red rash may appear on your skin.

a stinging nettle

Q: How does the stinging nettle sting?

A: It has tiny, hollow, needle-like tips on the leaves and stems. These can "inject" your skin with a stinging compound.

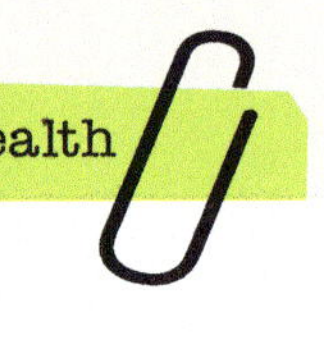

Life Science and Health

a stinging nettle caterpillar

The Stinging Nettle Caterpillar

Like the stinging nettle plant, the stinging nettle caterpillar can also give people painful stings if they touch its tiny, sharp spines.

It is mainly found in South-East Asia. However, in 2001, the first stinging nettle caterpillar was found in Hawaii. People are concerned about the discovery of the caterpillar because it could damage food crops there.

A Response from an Entomologist

An article appeared in Hawaii's *Maui News* on 24 September 2007. The article describes the discovery of the stinging nettle caterpillar in Hawaii. The caterpillar feeds on the grass, which means that pastures and pineapple fields can become infested. Mr Fukada, an entomologist, believes it is a concern because the infestation can become harder to control.

"One of the disturbing things about what we're seeing is that they're feeding on guinea grass. That means every pasture, every gulch, every pineapple field can be infested and that makes it harder to control," said Mr Fukuda.

Mr Fukada has done an excellent review of the situation. He has considered all of the main factors relating to this issue. His comments indicate that he has a good understanding of the problem and his recommendations provide a sound approach for reducing the problem.

It was a very thorough report and offered the reason for the infestation and what it will mean for agriculture in Hawaii. Hopefully scientists can use this information to stop the spread of the caterpillar.

Lethal Leaves!

Lethal Rhubarb Leaves

Rhubarb leaves must not be eaten. We can eat cooked rhubarb stalks in an apple and rhubarb pie – yum – but not the leaves!

Lethal Lily-of-the-Valley

Every part of the beautiful lily-of-the-valley plant is lethal.

rhubarb leaves

Watch Out for Berries!

Lethal Berries

Don't bite the berries below. They can make people very sick or even cause death.

- deadly nightshade berries
- daphne berries
- jasmine berries
- mistletoe tree berries

You may see birds eating these berries but that does not mean they are safe for people to eat.

mistletoe tree berries

daphne berries

deadly nightshade berries

Index

Glossary

antidote	A substance that stops a poison from harming a person
barbs	Small backward-pointing angles on a shaft that make a sting difficult to remove
biodiversity	The range of different living things in a particular area
entomologist	A scientist that studies insects and their behaviour
immune	Has a natural defence, or is not harmed by something
parasite	A living thing that needs to live on or inside another living thing in order to survive
plankton	Tiny plants that live in the ocean
super-organism	A living thing that is made up of many individual creatures